Hansel and Gretel

 Fairy Tale Treasury

Adapted by
Jane Jerrard

Illustrated by
Susan Shelburne

Publications International, Ltd.

Long ago, a poor woodcutter lived on the edge of a large forest with his wife and two children, named Hansel and Gretel. One autumn, there was no food in the land. The man could not feed his family.

The woodcutter's wife, who was the children's stepmother, warned that the whole family would soon die of hunger. One night she told her husband that he must take the children into the woods and leave them there.

But Hansel overheard this and he told Gretel. The children were both very frightened. Hansel made a plan. Later that night, when the moon was high, the boy sneaked out and gathered as many white pebbles as his pockets would hold.

The next day, the children went with their father to gather wood. As they walked into the woods, Hansel secretly dropped pebbles to mark the path.

Deep in the woods, the wood-cutter built a fire and left the children on their own with only some bread to eat. Hansel and Gretel slept for awhile. Then, with the moon shining on the white pebbles, they followed the path home. The stepmother pretended to be glad when she saw them, but she was secretly angry.

The next day, the woman told her husband to lead Hansel and Gretel back into the woods again.

This time, the woodcutter led them deeper into the forest. Hansel had no pebbles, so he crumbled his bread and left a trail of crumbs. Hansel and Gretel waited for the moon to rise, then they searched for the trail. But the bread had been eaten by birds, so they could not find their way home.

The next morning, Gretel saw a white bird that sang so sweetly they followed it down a path.

They followed the bird to a most amazing house. The house was made of gingerbread, with a roof of icing. The children each broke off a piece of the house and started to eat. No sooner had they filled their mouths than they heard a voice.

"Nibble, nibble like a mouse, who's that nibbling at my house?" the voice said.

The door opened, and there stood an ugly old woman.

The woman smiled and invited them inside. Seeing how hungry and tired they were, she gave them a wonderful dinner of apples and pancakes, then she put them to bed.

Hansel and Gretel did not know that the woman who seemed so nice was really a wicked witch! Before Hansel and Gretel awoke the next morning, the witch carried Hansel to a little cage she had built and she locked him inside.

"Now," she cackled, "I'll fatten him up and eat him!"

The witch made poor Gretel cook meals for Hansel, for she wanted him to grow plump. Hansel and Gretel begged to be set free, but the witch just laughed.

Each day, the witch asked to feel Hansel's finger. She couldn't see too well, so Hansel cleverly gave her an old bone to feel. The witch thought he was still too thin.

Weeks went by, and Hansel didn't seem to grow any fatter. The witch grew tired of waiting. One morning, the witch ordered Gretel to climb up into the oven to see if the fire was ready. But Gretel said, "How can I get into the oven?"

The witch climbed up to show Gretel how to look at the fire. Quick as a wink, Gretel gave the witch a shove that sent her tumbling all the way into the oven!

The children filled their pockets with the witch's treasures and set out for home. Before they had gone far, they came to the edge of a wide lake. Luckily, a swan agreed to carry them across the water. The two then found a path they knew.

The woodcutter cried tears of joy to see his children again. He had sent his wife away after he finally realized how wicked she was. The woodcutter and his children lived happily for the rest of their days... with the help of the witch's gold!